This Orchard book belongs to

_____

_____

_____

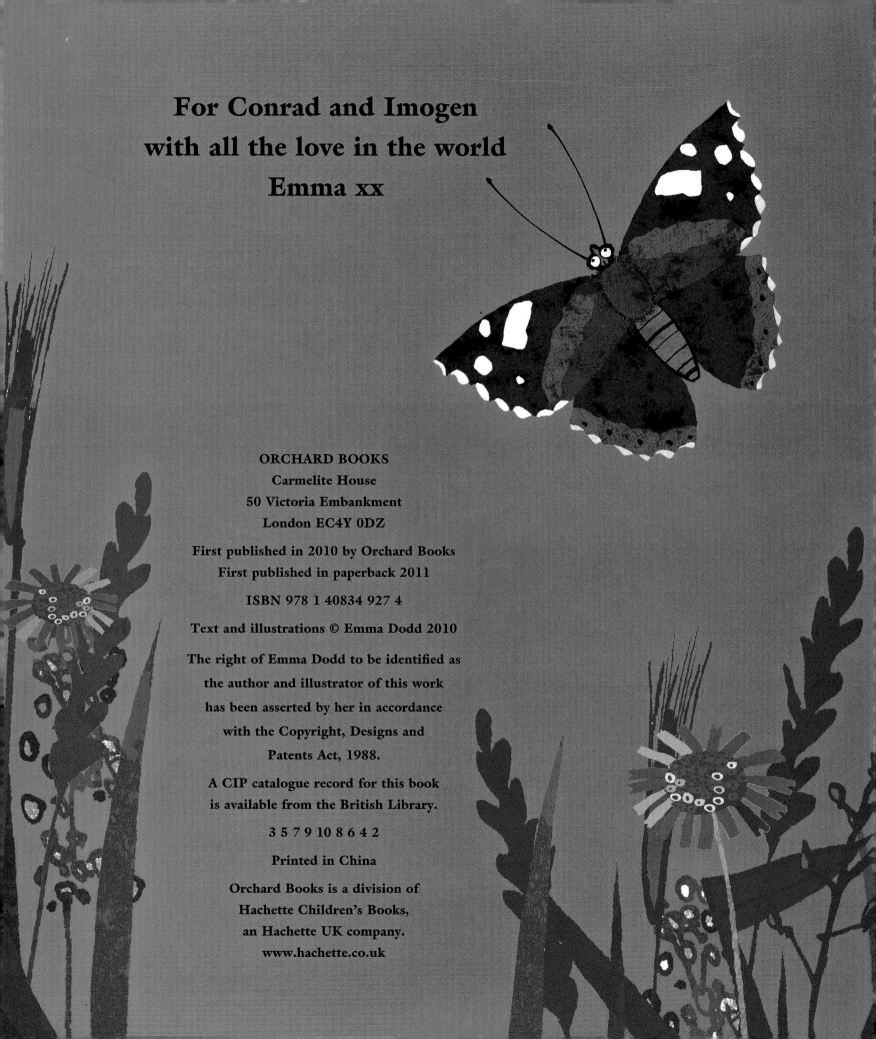

For Conrad and Imogen
with all the love in the world
Emma xx

ORCHARD BOOKS

Carmelite House

50 Victoria Embankment

London EC4Y 0DZ

First published in 2010 by Orchard Books

First published in paperback 2011

ISBN 978 1 40834 927 4

Text and illustrations © Emma Dodd 2010

The right of Emma Dodd to be identified as
the author and illustrator of this work
has been asserted by her in accordance
with the Copyright, Designs and
Patents Act, 1988.

A CIP catalogue record for this book
is available from the British Library.

3 5 7 9 10 8 6 4 2

Printed in China

Orchard Books is a division of
Hachette Children's Books,
an Hachette UK company.
www.hachette.co.uk

I love bugs!

Emma Dodd

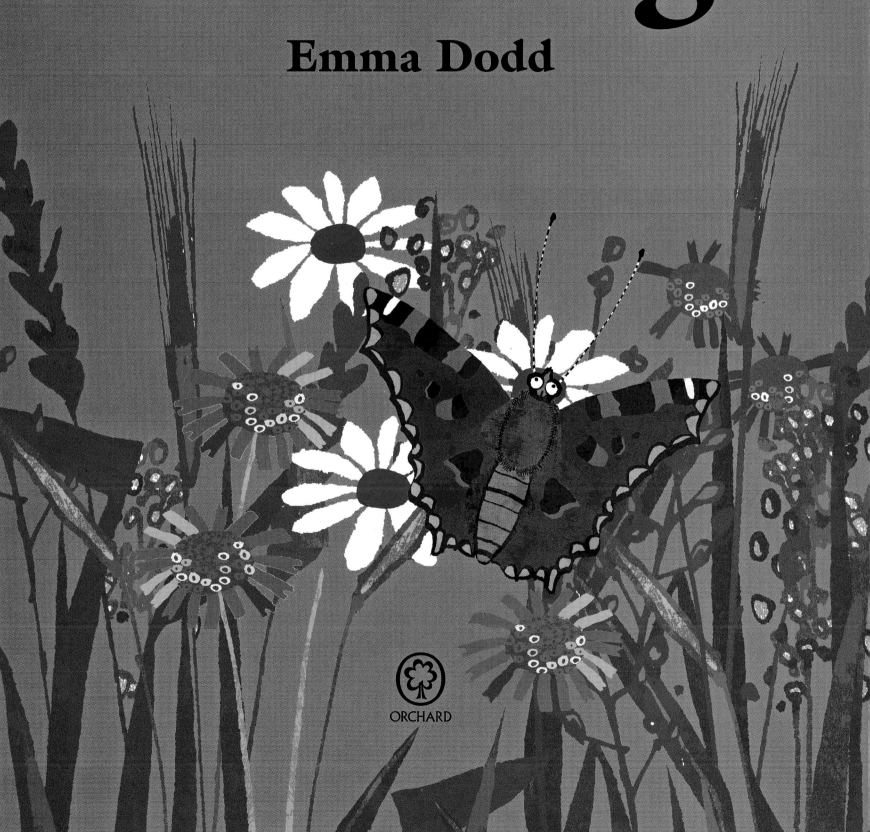

ORCHARD

I love all bugs...

big

and

small bugs.

I love springy

jumpy leapy
bugs

and
slimy
crawly
creepy
bugs.

I love hard spiky spiny bugs and pretty spotty shiny bugs.

I love fuzzy sunny honey bugs

and **furry**

whirry

funny

bugs.

I love brightly-coloured-wing bugs
and stripy swipey

sting bugs.

I love whiny buzzy

sound bugs

and glide-across-the-ground
bugs.

I love
flouncy

frilly

flutter
bugs

and silly clitter-clutter
bugs.

I love fly-around-the-light bugs and curl-up-tight bugs.

Yes, I love all bugs! Hop

and fly and crawl bugs.

But the best bugs are hairy bugs. Eight-legged scary bugs.

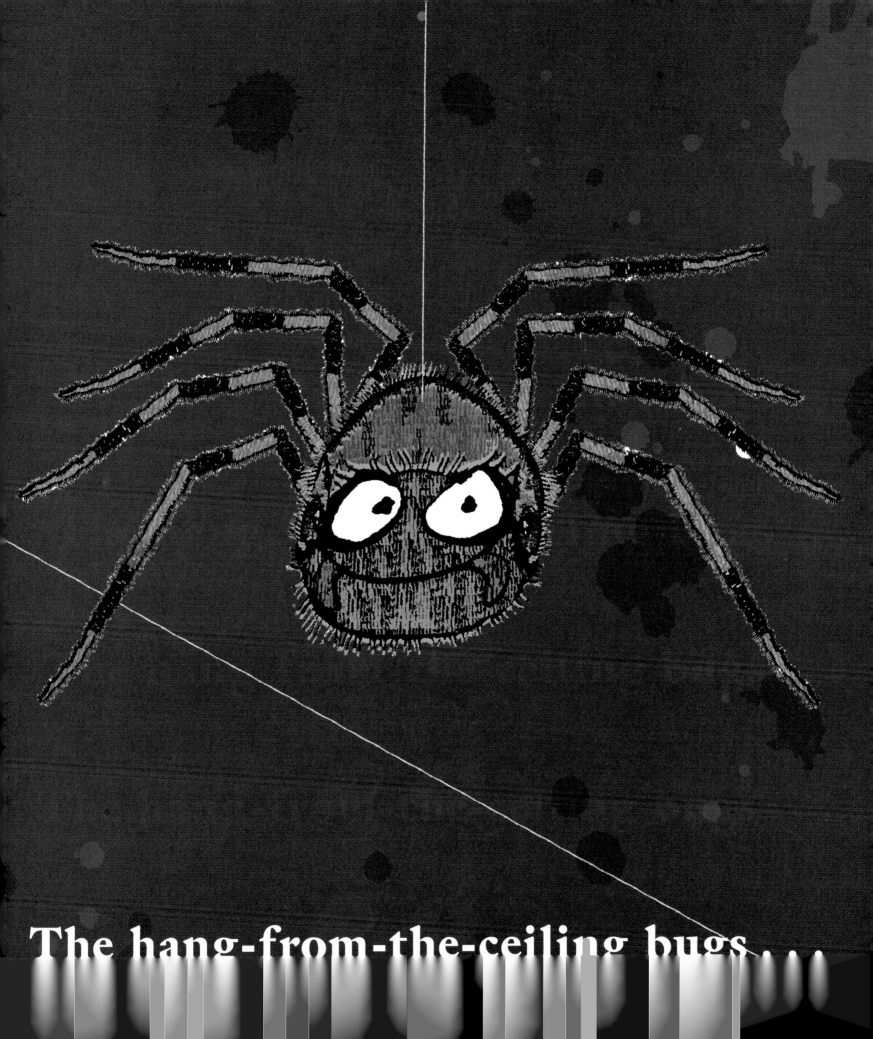

The hang-from-the-ceiling bugs . . .

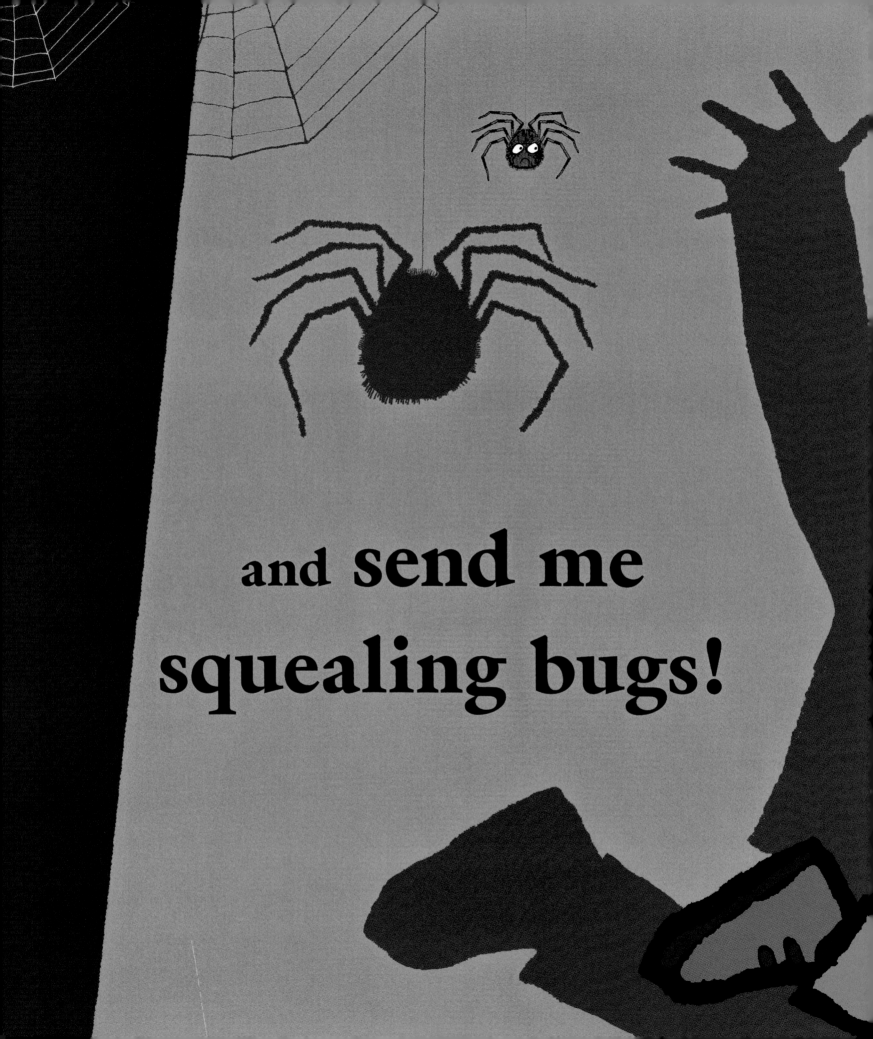

and **send me** squealing bugs!